Charlie Brown, Snoopy And Me

Charlie Brown, Snoopy And Me

And All the Other Peanuts Characters

Charles M. Schulz

with R. Smith Kiliper
conceived and produced by Whitehall, Hadlyme & Smith, Inc.

Doubleday & Company, Inc.
Garden City, New York

Library of Congress Catalog Card Number 80-923

ISBN: 0-385-15805-X Trade
ISBN: 0-385-15806-8 Prebound

Contents

Charlie Brown, Snoopy And Me

Children's fashions were something in those days. Here I am being held by my father.

1

In The Beginning

I was born Charles Monroe Schulz in Minneapolis, Minnesota, on November 26, 1922, but that name didn't stick with me very long. An uncle nicknamed me "Sparky" after a horse called "Sparkplug," who was a regular character in a comic strip at the time—"Barney Google." Cartoon strips were a part of my life almost from the day I was born.

When I was about four years old, I owned a small blackboard. There was a paper roll at the top on which the alphabet was printed. I think I knew my ABC's before I entered kindergarten. For years, that blackboard was my friend. I used it to draw hundreds of pictures, and for a pretend school blackboard. Probably that and a small rolltop desk were the two most valuable and important possessions of my childhood.

During the first week of kindergarten, the teacher handed out sheets of paper and boxes of crayons and told us to draw whatever we wanted. Since we were living in St. Paul at the time, I knew a little about snowstorms, so I decided to draw a man shoveling snow. Apparently it was quite a drawing. A few days before, my mother had received a letter from some relatives who had moved to Needles, California, which is desert country. I was so taken with their description of the scenery out there that I added a palm tree to my picture of the snowstorm. The teacher looked at it and said, "Some day, Charles, you're going to be an artist."

In 1930, my father, my mother and I moved to Needles, where we lived for a year before moving back to St. Paul. I often think of the nature of the relationship between my parents and me. There are times when I would like to go back to the years with my mother and father—the times when I could have them bear all my worries. It would be great to be able to go into the house where my mother was in the kitchen and my comic books were in the other room, and I could lie down on the couch and read the comics and then have dinner with my parents. The older I get, the more I miss my parents, but I realize that those days are gone forever.

Those old Fords were something,
and I always seemed to take
a package of Cracker Jack when I went for a ride.

That realization requires maturity.

I believe that one of the ways we learn in this life is to take the past and lay it over the present to see how they compare. This helps in my relationships with my own children. If you place yourself in that same age bracket and remember what you were thinking in those days, you begin to understand.

My father, Carl Schulz, was a man of great integrity, and a man who was well respected. Most people may look at the barbering business as being really nothing very important, but I look upon it as being a profession. To do what my father did— with only a third grade education, to go to

work on a Nebraska farm to save enough money to go to barber college—required a lot of character. At first, he had to go to work for somebody else and save more money; then he was able to buy his own establishment and build up his own business. That is really doing a lot with what you have. I always noticed that his barbershop was a clean, respectable place, with no raunchy characters throwing cigarette butts on the floor and telling dirty jokes. It was a place where women and children could come; it was a family barbershop, and he was proud of that.

I noticed that he was well respected by other members of his profession. The other barbers looked up to him, and sometimes they would call him "Senator." People would frequently say, "Schulz should have been a public official." I think that he would have been a good senator, but his background and lack of higher education prohibited this. He did, however, get involved in some barber legislation by which he helped to elevate the profession. I knew that people respected him.

Somehow, we survived the Great Depression of the 1930s. I know that it was very hard on him because he was conscientious. At one time, he was seven months

behind in his rent to the owner of the large building that the barbershop was in. I asked him about it years later: "Why did the fellow let you get seven months behind?" He said that it hadn't mattered, that most of the other stores and apartments had been just sitting there empty because there was no way to rent them out. I think that he paid seventy-five dollars a month rent for his place, and I suppose his weekly take-home pay was about fifty dollars. Fifty dollars a week during the Depression was pretty good, but he worked hard for it. I do know that he kept on journeyman barbers that he could easily have done without because he simply was too kindhearted to let them go.

My father influenced me in many ways, but one that stands out is his love for the funnies. Comic strips were very important entertainment in those days. People of my parents' age could remember the time when there were no radio programs for entertainment and the funnies rated high. I imagine he grew up reading the comics and just kept on with it. I know that his favorite strip as he grew older was "Mickey Finn." He loved it.

My mother, Dena Halverson Schulz, died when she was forty-eight, so I knew

Here I am on my one-speed tricycle.

her only during those years when kids take everything for granted. I saw her as being one of those people who are looked to for help by their brothers and sisters. Now that I am almost fifty-eight, and think of her as being ten years younger than I am now when she died, I can relate much more closely to the terror and the agony she must have gone through, dying that long, lingering death from cancer. I can understand the pain and fear she must have had, thinking about what was to become of me. It saddens me to know that I will never see her again and will never be able to talk about some of the things I

have been able to figure out about life as a parent.

I was a good student in elementary school. I received a diploma in the second grade for being the outstanding boy student, and I was promoted a half grade in the third grade, and once again in the fifth grade. By the time I was in the sixth grade, I was too far ahead of myself, and was the smallest and youngest kid in the class.

I never felt deprived while I was in elementary school. It seems to me that I always had the things I really wanted. I had a bicycle when I was twelve and had good baseball equipment, skates, hockey sticks, and all the things that I wanted. I also had a lot of comic books. In fact, for a while, I bought all the comic books that were published. I had the biggest collection of comic books and "Big Little Books" in the neighborhood.

I also ran around with a pretty decent group of guys, although I didn't have many friends in school, since school friends didn't mean much to me. To me, life began when school was out. My friends were the boys with whom I played ball or hockey. I have kept in contact with a couple of them and we still correspond.

During my years in elementary school, I

I still draw all the time.

drew all the time. Usually, I tried to copy the style of "Buck Rogers," one of my favorites, but I was also crazy about all of the Walt Disney characters and Popeye. I would draw Popeye and Mickey Mouse and the Three Little Pigs on the covers of my notebooks, and the other kids would see them and say, "Hey, would you draw Popeye on my book?" So, I'd have to sit there and draw Popeye on the notebooks of all the other kids.

Actually, I don't really know if I was aware that there were such things as comic strip artists. I liked the funny papers and I was fascinated by them and read every one, but I suppose I didn't realize that you could make a living drawing until I was in my early teens. Generally, comic strips were regarded as a very low form of art and something not worthy of a person's ambition.

Then came junior high school and the collapse of the academic roof. In the tenth grade I failed everything in sight. For a time, high school was not much better. I think I must have won the award for being the most miserable physics student in the entire history of St. Paul Central High School. It took three years to get back on the track, but I finally graduated when I was seventeen, right on schedule.

Those were hard years. It is difficult to overcome the belief that you really don't know anything and are truly stupid. I suppose that is the basis for a lot of the problems that kids have in school—the dread of being called upon, the fear of knowing that you are going to have to recite when you really don't know the answer, the watching of the clock, hoping it will hurry up so the bell will ring and you won't have to be called upon to read the paper that you know is inadequate.

All this time, however, I was drawing. I didn't always have my own room, so my mother let me use the dining room table. She had a beautiful tablecloth that she had crocheted, and I had to make sure that I folded it carefully and put it aside so that I wouldn't spill ink on it.

I did a lot of copying in those days. One of my inspirations was Roy Crane, who drew "Wash Tubbs and Captain Easy." He may have received little credit from lay-men, but he inspired more cartoonists than any other artist. He had a rollicking style of drawing that was marvelous.

I would also draw characters out of "Tim Tyler's Luck," another popular strip of the day. I liked the animals that were in the strip—lions, black panthers, etc.

I remember well a fateful trip to the St. Paul Public Library. They were exhibiting a large number of original comic strips, so my mother and my father took me over one Sunday to look at them. I saw how beautifully they were rendered, the size they were drawn, and how nicely they all were done. I went home and tore up all of my drawings and started over again.

In high school, I discovered the Sherlock Holmes stories. I bought scrapbooks and filled them with my own illustrations of that great detective. One of the people who liked those books the most was a friend of mine named Shermy. When I started "Peanuts," I used his name for one of the characters.

One evening, my mother showed me an ad in the paper which read, "Do you like to draw? Send for our free talent test." The ad was placed by a Minneapolis correspondence school which was known at the time as "Federal Schools" and later as "Art Instruction Schools, Inc." I decided to enter because the school emphasized cartooning. The course cost one hundred seventy dollars, and I have always been thankful to my father for making the payments even though, I believe, it put him into debt.

While taking the correspondence course, I also had my first job as a delivery boy for a small grocery store. Although I was good at delivering groceries, I was useless as a clerk in the store, as I never knew the price of anything; thus, the job was a total disaster.

Most of my friends and I became caddies at Highland Park Golf Course, and we got quite good at it. The most we could ever earn, however, was about a dollar for eighteen holes. Our rate was seventy-five

Practicing a chip shot. Even then I was able to keep my eye on the ball.

cents, and if a golfer had an especially good round, he might give us a tip.

Later, I got a job working for two different direct mail advertisers and a printing company. My main duties were working in the office as an office boy, sweeping the floor, wrapping packages and delivering them.

When I later worked for Associated Letter Service and they discovered that I knew how to draw, I did some advertising drawings for them on their mimeograph machine. They were lucky. They were getting a wrapper, a delivery boy and an artist for sixteen dollars a week. Then I was drafted and that blew the whole thing.

I entered the Army in 1943, while my mother was suffering so much from fatal cancer. Fortunately, for the first few weeks of my Army life, I was stationed at Fort Snelling, Minnesota, just across the river from St. Paul. That meant that when I had a weekend pass I could go home.

One Sunday evening I went to say good-bye to my mother, as I had to get back to camp. She was lying in bed. She looked up at me and said, "I suppose that we should say good-bye, because we probably never will see each other again." The next day she died. I was only twenty at the time, and it saddens me that this wonderful woman who encouraged my drawing so much never lived to see any of my work in print.

I spent most of my Army time in Camp Campbell, Kentucky. I started off thinking that I could get into some sort of art work, but there seemed to be no need for anyone like me, since, at the time, I was still just an amateur. Now and then, the first sergeant had me paint little signs that were needed around the company area. When he needed someone to letter a sign that read "Latrine," I was the one they called upon. The truth is, I abandoned drawing during those years of my Army service. Although I carried a sketchbook

Once in a while I did sketch
a bit when I was in the Army.

around with me, I never used it a great
deal. I became more interested in trying to
be a good soldier, and especially in trying
to be a good light-machinegun squad
leader. I believe I was a good soldier, as I
did what I was supposed to do, and I did it
reasonably well.

I also learned what it is to be lonely in the
Army, and I know that much of that feeling
has been inflicted upon Charlie Brown. We
were lonely, we were anxious, and the fact
that the war was still on meant that none of
us ever knew how long we would be in
service. There was no end to the war in
sight, and we thought that we might be

I even made sergeant.

soldiers for the rest of our lives.

When I returned from the Army, I tried to get a job in art departments almost everywhere in the Twin Cities of Minneapolis and St. Paul, but no one wanted me. Well, actually, I *was* almost hired by a man who was looking for someone to letter tombstones. Fortunately, he changed his mind about me. I was worried about how I would have explained that job to my friends.

I decided to take my sample portfolio to *Timeless Topix*, a Catholic comic magazine. Roman Baltes, the art director, handed me some comic strips which had already been drawn, but still had empty balloons, and asked me to do the lettering on a free-lance basis.

A few weeks later, I was hired by my old alma mater, Art Instruction Schools, Inc., as an instructor. I frequently got up early in the morning, traveled to *Timeless Topix* in downtown St. Paul, left my lettering work, then went to Minneapolis to work at Art Instruction Schools. In the evening after work, I would go home and stay up until midnight doing my lettering for *Timeless Topix*. The next morning, the routine started all over again.

My free-lance work for *Timeless Topix* expanded and I began lettering the balloons in French and Spanish. The problem was, I didn't have any idea of what I was lettering. Then something important happened. *Timeless Topix* decided to run a page of gag cartoons that I had drawn. Although they thought better of it after two appearances, I had come up with an idea for using tiny kids as subjects for panel cartoons, and I made my first appearance in print as a comic artist. Even though there was a similarity between those drawings and the drawings that I do now, I must confess that, at the time, I had only a

meager interest in drawing little kids. I drew them because they were what sold.

Frank Wing, a friend at Art Instruction, suggested that I draw samples of my cartoon kids and take them to the St. Paul *Pioneer Press*. I did, calling the panels "Li'l Folks," and the paper bought them. The

One of my first "Li'l Folks" panels. Notice the two characters that eventually grew up to be Charlie Brown and Snoopy.

strip became a weekly feature that ran for two years in the women's section.

I was also using some of my spare time to draw cartoons for magazines, but no one seemed to be interested. Finally, I clicked with *The Saturday Evening Post*. The first acceptance that I received from them took me by surprise. Their letter read, "Check Tuesday for spot drawing of boy on lounge." I had drawn a boy who was sitting at the end of a very long chaise longue with his feet on an unnecessary footstool. I thought the letter meant that the cartoon had been rejected and that I should check the mail on Tuesday to retrieve my drawing. But, no, it meant that they were going to pay me. From 1948 to 1950, I sold fifteen cartoons to *The Saturday Evening Post*.

In 1950, I sent a batch of samples to United Feature Syndicate in New York. Weeks went by and I decided that the package had been lost in the mail, so I wrote a letter of inquiry. I received a reply from Jim Freeman, the editorial director, who invited me to New York to talk over my work. The morning of my appointment, I got to their offices before most of the people had arrived. I brought with me a new comic strip I had been working on, rather than more samples of "Li'l Folks." I left the strip with the receptionist and went out for breakfast. By the time I returned, the United Feature Syndicate folks had already decided that they liked the strip better than the panels. The whole thing was underway.

For some reason, the most important result of my new-found success seemed to be that I was now able to buy a new car. Up

CHARLES SCHULZ

THE SATURDAY EVENING POST

My first *Saturday Evening Post* cartoon. Reprinted from *The Saturday Evening Post*.
© 1948 The Curtis Publishing Company.

to that time, cars had never interested me. When I was a kid, once you got to be fifteen years old, you just had to go downtown, get weighed, fill out a form and give the people thirty-five cents to get your driver's license the following week. Then, you could drive legally—that's all there was to it. My dad had let me use his 1934 Ford anytime I wanted to. It was no big deal. Since I was not a wild kid, there were no problems, but it had never occurred to me that I could own a car myself. After the war, I had gone back to driving my dad's car, which I later bought from him. It didn't have a radio, and the heater never worked too well, but it was a car.

With my new contract, and the promise of a steady income, I bought the first new car that anyone in our family had ever owned, a 1950 Ford, and it was a beauty. It was not a stripped-down economy model, for I had decided that if I were going to get a car, I would get the very best. What a thrill! It had a good heater and even a radio. It was wonderful. I loved the color, too. To me, it was a lime green, but some of my friends kidded me by calling it chartreuse.

At the time, my dad and I lived in an apartment where there was no garage, so I had to park my car on the street. I remember that when I would get home after dark, park the car and walk to the apartment building, I would always turn around to look back at my car, shining under the streetlights, and be so proud. Since then, I've had a whole bunch of cars, and they really don't mean anything anymore.

2
The Peanuts Characters

Today, "Peanuts" appears in about two thousand newspapers all over the world, has been translated into numerous languages, and is read by approximately 100 million people daily. More than 80 million people have bought the books. The "Peanuts" characters have been on television, in movies and on the Broadway stage. Some of them have appeared on the covers of *Time, Life, Newsweek, Paris Match, Le Magazine, Littéraire, Woman's Day, The Saturday Review, TV Guide* and *San Francisco* magazine, but the whole thing didn't start out that grandly.

When I submitted my ideas to United Feature Syndicate, I wanted to continue using my original title, "Li'l Folks." We found, however, that an artist named Tack Knight had been drawing a strip called "Little Folks," and even though he was no

Here's the beginning of "Peanuts." Shermie, Patty and

longer drawing it, he wanted to keep the title on the off chance he might use it later.

Since I wasn't able to come up with any great titles that were appropriate, United Feature Syndicate prepared a list of about ten titles, one of which was "Peanuts." I disliked the name then, as I do now, but in spite of my objection, they liked it; thus, the strip was named "Peanuts." I knew that people would think that "Peanuts" was the name of the lead character, and I was right. I used to get letters from people saying, "I liked the strip yesterday when Peanuts was feeding his dog." That always made me

Charlie Brown were born on October 2, 1950.

angry. Peanuts is not a word that describes children, but one that describes something that is insignificant or unworthy. Nevertheless, I was told, "No, Peanuts is a title that will catch the eye of potential newspaper subscribers." So, who was I, an unknown kid from St. Paul, to argue with them? I gave in.

At any rate, the strip appeared for the first time on October 2, 1950, in a grand total of nine newspapers. During the first year, the number of newspapers carrying the strip increased to thirty-five; there were forty-five the following year. A year later, I

Lucy and Peppermint Patty became friends.

Sunday page, which first appeared on January 6, 1952.

When the first strip appeared in 1950, there were only four characters: Charlie Brown, Snoopy, Shermy and Patty (not Peppermint Patty). At the time, I was not sure who the main characters were going to be. The cast increased in number as time went on. Schroeder appeared in 1951, Lucy and Linus in 1952, Sally Brown (Charlie Brown's sister) in 1959, Frieda in 1961, Franklin in 1968, Woodstock in 1970 and Marcie in 1971. Shermy and Patty, half of the original cast, have almost

Over the years, Lucy became a bit melodramatic.

disappeared. The strip has changed so much since the beginning that I can use Shermy only when I need a character who has very little personality, one who will not mislead the reader. Besides, I never liked the way I drew Shermy. He never came out right. I was not even satisfied with the way I drew his hair.

I was lucky that "Peanuts" started when it did. The days of popular adventure strips were waning, probably because television had become such a dominating medium.

I have never regarded children as my main audience. The real fans are adults,

from high school age on up, for they have memories of what it was like to be a child, and can appreciate "Peanuts" much more deeply than can the youngsters. Naturally, our childhood memories fade as we grow up. It's a matter of protection. I have a theory that I call "removal of the lids." We are all pretty much what we are going to be early in our lives. Our personalities and characteristics are established, usually, by the time we are five or six years old, but the lids are on. We are like boiling pots on a stove, and when we are small, the adults keep the lids on.

As children, we cannot express ourselves the way we would like to, but as we grow older, the lids pop off, and the characteristics come out. We also discover ways to protect ourselves—to no longer be put into the positions of fear and anxiety that we are forced to be in as children. As children, we are forced to go to school, to be in a room with thirty other kids, to do things we don't want to do or that will make fools of us. When we become adults, we make sure that we no longer get trapped. Unfortunately, this also robs us of many wonderful adventures. Perhaps "Peanuts" is a way of returning to childhood and yet not being exposed to its unpleasantness.

Very little material used in the strip has

Sometimes it's tough growing up.

come from observations of real children. I may have borrowed a few ideas from my own children when they were small, but now that they are grown, I no longer have the opportunity. I don't mean that I actually stole specific ideas from them, but I did borrow broad themes such as Linus and his security blanket and Lucy being a fussbudget. There were probably fewer than a dozen actual ideas, however, that the kids provided me in the thirty years I have been drawing "Peanuts."

This does not mean that there was not an inspiration somewhere in the back-

Charlie Brown—the consummate loser.

ground as I observed the relationships between children, but far more of the strip depends on my own observations and memories than it does on the actual present-day experiences in my family.

Some of my best ideas have come from a mood of sadness, rather than a feeling of well-being. Strangely enough, pleasant things are not really funny. You can't create humor out of happiness. I'm astonished at the number of people who write to me saying, "Why can't you create happy stories for us? Why does Charlie Brown always have to lose? Why can't you

let him kick the football?'' Well, there is nothing funny about the person who gets to kick the football. Drama and humor come from trouble and sadness, and mankind's astounding ability to survive life's unhappiness. It is a virtual miracle that we have existed over these millions of years against such deplorable odds, when everything is against us.

I have found that inspiration is almost impossible to describe. Some things that appear in the strip are unconnectable to the original inspiration, even if I talk about it. Any event that I attend can provide some kind of inspiration. I can almost guarantee that if I attend a symphony concert and see a violinist perform as the soloist in a concerto, or if I merely watch a great conductor, my mind will begin to churn up all sorts of ideas that will have no relationship to watching a violinist or a conductor, but there will be an inspiration there.

A big breakthrough for my strip was its appearance in foreign newspapers. Although I have no idea in how many countries the strip appears, I do know that, as of now, there are about one hundred thirty-seven book collections published in Denmark, Sweden, Italy, Belgium, England, Germany, Iceland, Switzerland, Japan, Brazil, France and South Africa.

Just a couple of "Peanuts" translations in Spanish . . .

As far as translation is concerned, I can't worry too much about that, for I don't speak any foreign languages very well. I do know that there are many language problems involved in translation because there are certain words and thoughts that really cannot be translated. Overcoming this barrier is the problem of the translator.

For example, when Snoopy is eating and remarks, "Scarf city!", there is no way this really can be translated unless one has an excellent knowledge of at least two languages. The implications of the term must be known in American English; then a word must be found in another language which is equivalent to "scarfing" junk food and the word must be used in slang form. I've had to stop worrying about people

and Japanese.

understanding me in a foreign language. Some people in a foreign country may understand the meaning of a translation, while others in the same country do not. As a matter of fact, I'm sure there are people in the United States who don't understand me.

Here is another example of what can happen when a comic strip is translated.

At one time, there was an Italian communist newspaper, *L'Unita,* that attacked "Peanuts" for its "alienating and alienated ideology." Just a few blocks away, another left-wing Italian paper, *Paese Sera,* was running the strip on its pages without comment. At the same time, *The Moscow News* was running it daily, but without copyright permission.

"A Charlie Brown Christmas," our first television show, appeared on December 9, 1965. This program, produced by Lee Mendelson and animated by Bill Melendez, drew 50 per cent of the viewing audience in the United States, won both an Emmy and a Peabody Award, and is still repeated every year. Since that time, we have collaborated on more than twenty other "Peanuts" specials.

The voices used in the shows are those of very young children. We audition new girls and boys every two years, because as these child actors grow, their voices change and become too mature. One exception to this rule is the voice of Snoopy, which has always been done by Bill Melendez.

On March 7, 1967, the musical *You're A Good Man, Charlie Brown* opened, starring, as Charlie Brown, Gary Burghoff, who later went on to fame in the role of Radar in M*A*S*H*. The play ran for four years in New York and there were nine touring companies, both in the United States and abroad. It has been the most performed musical in the history of the American theater and even was shown on television as a "Hallmark Hall of Fame" production. I have seen photographs of the cast who performed in a Copenhagen production; they were amusing because the fellow who played Linus was over six feet tall, an enormous man. I've seen the play performed with girls playing Snoopy and even Charlie Brown, but no matter how they do the play, it survives.

The "Peanuts" characters also appeared in a feature-length film, *A Boy Named Charlie Brown,* which opened at Radio City Music Hall in New York on December 11, 1969. Since then, four other feature-length films have been made.

Perhaps the most unusual thing that has happened was the involvement of Charlie Brown and Snoopy with the Apollo 10 Lunar Expedition in 1969. This space shot was not programmed to land on the moon. The astronauts' mission was to orbit the moon, test the separating of the lunar module from the spacecraft, bring the two together again, and redock.

That's the Emmy Award right in the middle of my office. (Catherine Kiliper photo)

The men involved were Navy Commander Eugene A. Cernan, Air Force Colonel Thomas P. Stafford and Navy Commander John W. Young. They nicknamed the command module "Charlie Brown" and the lunar module "Snoopy." John Young held up a picture of Snoopy during the fourth telecast, when the Apollo 10 mission was halfway to the moon, one hundred ten thousand miles away from earth, but the good news was to come later. When the joyous moment came that the spacecraft and the lunar module had been successfully redocked, the report came back over the radio to mission control, "Snoopy and Charlie Brown are hugging each other."

Hardly anyone loses 600–0, but, as usual, it's Charlie Brown's fault.

3

The Games Peanuts Play

Sports have always been important in "Peanuts." All of the characters play baseball, Snoopy is a hockey nut and Charlie Brown tries to kick a football. Of course, all of that activity comes from my longtime interest in sports.

Athletics were always important to us as kids, but when you live in Minnesota, you get used to short seasons. In the spring, we played marbles. I was a pretty good marble player when I was young. I had two shooters that just fit my fingers, and I kept them for years. Recently, they disappeared—I don't have any idea what happened to them. That's very aggravating. I also had about six hundred other marbles that I had saved since I was ten, in a big cigar box. I was very proud of them. Then I made the mistake of letting my own kids play with them. How you can lose six hundred

44

Woodstock is a football fan, too . . .

marbles is beyond me.

When summer came, our sport was baseball. Since Little League had not yet been invented, we organized our own teams and challenged other neighborhood teams. There were no good fields for us to use, and the ball took strange hops. There were times when we had to pry up manhole covers to let someone go below to rescue the ball when it had fallen through the street drain into the sewer. Baseball is a great sport to use in the strip.

As well as a real swinger.

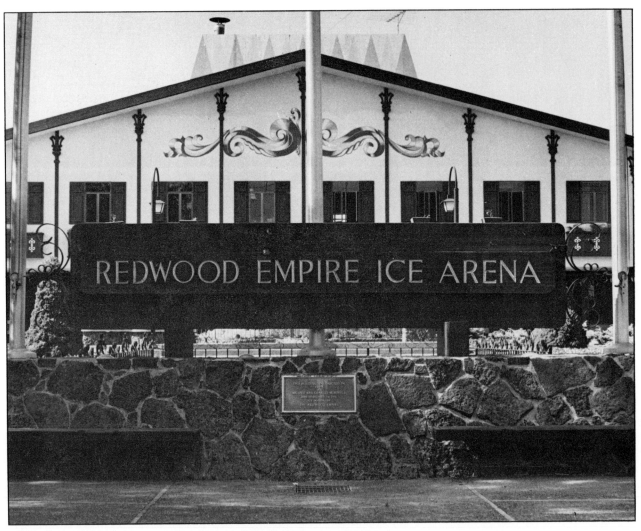

"Snoopy's Home Ice," our own rink. (R. Smith Kiliper photo)

One of the signatures outside the rink. (R. Smith Kiliper photo)

Here is the world-famous hockey player. (R. Smith Kiliper photo)

Hockey can be tiring.

Sometimes I do a bit of refereeing.

(David French photo)

But I often get out on the ice.

Snoopy took up tennis at about the same time that my wife, Jeannie, and I did and he seems to have the same problems that I do.

I can have those long discussions on the pitcher's mound and the topic doesn't necessarily have to be about baseball.

I never had a favorite major league baseball team. As kids, we never cared about the Yankees, the Cubs, the Giants or any other big-league club. We lived in St. Paul, and were much more interested in the St. Paul Saints and the Minneapolis Millers. Who cared about Joe DiMaggio? The Saints were our heroes.

Charlie Brown and I both have face faces.

4

Charlie Brown

Charlie Brown first appeared—minus a name—in 1947. He was a character in my "Li'l Folks" cartoons and he also appeared in my *Saturday Evening Post* panels. Actually, he is a product of those magazines. Magazine cartooning is different from comic strip cartooning, since it uses greater exaggeration. This was especially true back in the 1940s, when kids were drawn with tiny bodies and huge heads. You only need a character for one idea, and the character, in most cases, doesn't have to be doing much. He or she is just standing there. Anyway, that's how Charlie Brown was born.

I like to think of Charlie Brown as being a bit of Everyman. Most people would admit to often feeling a bit like him—some of us more often than others. He tries to assume a perfect social image, but every-

Charlie Brown's life is a struggle. He can't even get a decent job.

thing seems to go wrong. There is a lot of myself in his character, too.

When I was little, I was so convinced that I had a very plain face that I was surprised when anyone recognized me. My idea was to give Charlie Brown a face with very little character. Despite all of my practice, he remains the most difficult to draw of all the kids. I guess it's the roundness of his head.

But sometimes Charlie Brown causes his own problems.

Sometimes you just can't win.

As I mentioned, when the "Peanuts" strip started, there were only four characters and I was not sure who would become the hero or heroine. I had trouble deciding because, at the time, Charlie Brown was not the put-upon character that he is now. Eventually I had trouble making Shermy anything but a straight man; Patty and a new girl, Violet, were serving merely as straight women; and Snoopy hadn't started thinking yet—so all the good lines were given to Charlie Brown.

As the years went on, he changed from a flippant little guy to the loser we all know. His appearance changed, too. His face matured a little and by the mid-1960s he looked as he does now.

He is always the one who receives the final blow or brings disaster on his friends. He is always the one who suffers—but doesn't everyone suffer from time to time? I like to think that all of his readers can sympathize with him since everybody has had experiences in losing. Only one person can win, but the rest have to lose. Besides, what's so funny about winning?

Charlie Brown's daily life is a struggle, and we can empathize with him, since he is the person that everything bad seems to happen to. He is likable, however, and would probably make a good friend. He's decent and kind. He never gives up trying to fly his kite, win a baseball game or kick a football. Who hasn't felt like Charlie Brown after a bad day?

Even after his worst days, though, in a way, he triumphs over adversity. He realizes, like the rest of us, that it is amazing how rapidly things can turn around, going from bad to good. Even his fans try to help him out of the dumps. That's what friends are for.

Every time "It's the Great Pumpkin,

Charlie Brown" is shown on television, for example, something happens. On the show, Charlie Brown gets only rocks in his "trick or treat" bag, and people all over the country send bags of candy to our studio for me to give to him. Or when "Be My Valentine, Charlie Brown" is telecast, and Charlie Brown gets not one single valentine, hundreds of his admirers send him love notes.

Unrequited love is one of the main themes of the "Peanuts" strip.

I have always thought that the challenge of sports is a caricature of the challenges in everyday life. I get a lot of ideas for the strip after a disastrous bowling night, a horrendous set of tennis, a below-par hockey game or a bad evening playing bridge.

I distinctly remember an afternoon when I was a kid and my friends and I went out after school to play a scheduled baseball game. The memory of our forty-to-nothing loss is still vivid. It stayed with me so long that I am sure that this game was the basis of Charlie Brown's uninterrupted string of losses. I know what it means to be totally wiped out in a sport by either an individual or another team.

A lot of my ideas come from things that happened to me when I was young. I remember standing in line for what

seemed to be hours in front of a St. Paul movie theater. They had advertised that the first five hundred kids in line for the Saturday matinee would get a free Butterfinger candy bar. When my turn came to step up to the box office, I was informed that they had run out of candy. I must have been the five hundred and first kid in line. Not so oddly, many years later, the same thing happened to Charlie Brown.

There have been other, much stranger, inspirations for Charlie Brown's troubles. I can't explain this, but I think that the whole business about Charlie Brown and his inability to speak to the little red-haired girl was really suggested to me by a Joni James album in which she sang some heartrending tune by Hank Williams.

A stained-glass window at the ice rink, showing our championship skater. (Catherine Kiliper photo)

5

Snoopy

Snoopy (also known as Snobben in Sweden, Sniff in Norway, and Snupijeve in Yugoslavia), like Charlie Brown, came from the "Li'l Folks" cartoons. In the beginning, he looked just like a dog, but his growth over the years has been strange.

I've always had a fondness for dogs, although I'm also a little afraid of them. I have no desire to be bitten, so I am leery about dogs who come charging up to me barking loudly.

I've noticed this about dogs. When you are walking down the sidewalk or the street and you happen to meet a dog coming the other way, as you pass him, the dog will look up at you. He may keep his head down, but he will always glance at you when he passes. He has to make sure that you are not going to hit him on the head or

At times, Snoopy can be a lot smarter than other members of the gang.

kick him as he goes by. I soon resolved that Snoopy would never worry about things like that.

I have always thought that there were a lot of dogs that were smarter than their young masters, so I decided to let Snoopy "think." That made him superior to any other cartoon dog. Letting Snoopy think and walk around on his hind legs also made him superior to the kids in the strip, since he could go his own way and exhibit an imagination that was unmatched by the rest of the characters. It has been difficult to keep him from becoming the real hero of the strip. Maybe he has.

We have a golden retriever now, but the first dog I ever had was a Boston bull named Snooky. She got run over by a taxicab when she was about ten years old and I was about twelve. Her death was quite a shock. I can still remember the Sunday morning when I heard my dad come home from the veterinarian and tell somebody outside the door that Snooky was dead.

About a year later we got a dog named Spike, and he was the inspiration for Snoopy. He was the smartest and most uncontrollable dog that I have ever seen. Spike was a black-and-white mixed breed. What breeds they were, we never figured out, although there was probably a little hound and a little pointer in him. He had black ears and similar markings to Snoopy. One day I counted up and realized that Spike had a vocabulary of at least fifty words. You could say to him, "Spike, do you want a potato? Why don't you go downstairs and get a potato?" and he would immediately go down to the basement and stick his head in the potato sack and bring up a potato.

He also taught himself to ring the back doorbell to be let into the house. He would jump up and bang the doorbell until someone let him in. His biggest thrill was to ride in the car. Every Saturday night, at about nine, he would begin looking up at my dad. Remember that my father and I had a common love—the comic strips. After we had read them, we would discuss what was going to happen next to our heroes. So the Sunday comics were eagerly anticipated at our house. The two Sunday Minneapolis papers were off the press in time for us to pick them up at the drugstore at about nine on Saturday evenings. Just about that time, Spike would put his paws on the arms of my dad's chair to remind him that it was time to get the papers and, incidentally, give him a ride in the car. He never got the wrong day.

On weekday evenings, he would sit on the front porch with his head up against the screen door and look down the street for my dad's car. When he saw it turn the corner a full block away, he would go tearing through the house—rugs flying every which way—run out the back door and jump up and down behind the fence until my dad got out of the car. He was never satisfied until my dad rolled up the evening paper and handed it to him. Then he would proudly enter the house to deliver the paper to us.

Spike slept in a wicker clothes basket in the hallway and liked to have a blanket over him. We would cover him up at night and he would lie there and sleep until morning. He would get up and drag the blanket into the kitchen and crawl with it under our old four-legged stove until my dad came in. Then he would mooch part of my father's breakfast.

Spike would never drink out of a water

In this strip from 1959, I was obviously thinking of my old dog, Spike.

pan. The only place he would drink was in the bathroom. Spike would put one paw up on the sink and stand there until someone came in and turned on the water for him. Then he would drink right out of the faucet. He demanded cold running water. There was a lot of Snoopy in him.

Spike's eating habits led to my first published drawing. I dashed off a cartoon of the dog and sent it, with an explanation, to the Ripley "Believe It or Not" panel in the newspapers. "A hunting dog that eats pins, tacks and razor blades is owned by C. F. Schulz, St. Paul, Minn." Next to the drawing was a label with a little arrow pointing to Spike, with the notation, "Drawn by Sparky." I was fifteen years old and was now a published "artist." I patterned Snoopy after Spike and, many years later, when I introduced Snoopy's

Snoopy, like Spike, is something of a gourmet.

moustached brother, I had to call him Spike.

At first, I had decided to call my original little beagle "Sniffy." But just before the strip was to start publication, I accidentally saw a comic book on a newsstand. It was about a dog named Sniffy. So the name "Snoopy" was born.

Not long ago I was looking through a book on the movies and, lo and behold, there was a list of names that had been suggested and rejected for the names of the seven dwarfs in *Snow White.* They were Scrappy, Hoppy, Dirty, Dumpy, Hungry, Thrifty, Weepy, Doleful, Awful, Gabby, Flabby, Shifty, Helpful, Crabby, Daffy, Puffy, Chesty, Busy, Biggy, Gaspy and Snoopy. I'm glad that Disney decided not to use the name Snoopy.

We had a bit of a problem with Snoopy

Who knows?
Someday he may
win the championship.

when we were preparing for the first of our television specials. In the strip, Snoopy doesn't talk, he just thinks in balloons. So we had to stick with letting him do everything in pantomime, with a bit of huffing and puffing, an occasional whine and, once in a while, a little giggle.

The play, *You're a Good Man, Charlie Brown,* proved that a person could act like Snoopy without even being dressed like a dog. When the curtain opened, the audience saw a young man dressed in jeans and a white turtleneck sweater and tennis shoes, lying on top of a doghouse. As soon as he would say his first line in the play—"It is, indeed, a dog's life"— people immediately would start to applaud because they realized that this was Snoopy and they were willing to suspend disbelief for the next hour and a half. To them, that

Talk about being an egotist.

Snoopy does try to be polite.

The world-famous punster at work.

Snoopy isn't the only one who can make puns.

He does have dignity, but things have a way of backfiring.

young man in the white turtleneck really was a beagle.

People have asked me how Snoopy is able to sleep on top of his doghouse without falling off. The answer is simple. Birds can sleep standing on tree limbs because their brains send a message to their feet, activating a certain muscle that tightens their claws. Snoopy's brain sends a message to his ear muscles, which lock him to the top of the doghouse.

Snoopy in cement. (R. Smith Kiliper photo)

I just can't resist holding him on my lap. (R. Smith Kiliper photo)

Even when she first appeared, Lucy was making life miserable for Charlie Brown.

6
Lucy

Lucy has been holding a football for Charlie Brown for more than twenty years, and for more than twenty years she has been yanking it away at the last minute so that Charlie Brown falls on his back. She is not being mean—she just can't control herself. I have talked to football players who admit that, at times when their team was way ahead of their opponents, they had this tremendous desire to do the same thing, and one of them admitted that he actually did it when he was playing college ball.

Lucy can best be described as a fuss-budget. We all know people who are fussy and are always complaining about something, so Lucy is the one who fills that role when I need a crabby person. Her basic personality also helps me to create ideas. That's helpful, because a character's

Lucy the fussbudget.

Lucy the liberated woman.

Lucy's method of dealing with Snoopy.

personality brings ideas to a cartoonist as often as the cartoonist brings ideas to the personality.

Lucy and Linus are the only characters who have tiny half circles around their eyes. Charlie Brown and Snoopy have them when they are confused or surprised, but Lucy and Linus always look as if their eyes were slightly out of focus.

Over the years, Lucy has calmed down a bit. Perhaps it started when we began doing the television shows. She was supposed to be one of the stars of the first one, but she turned out to be too aggressive and abrasive. She just did not sound good screaming all the time. She was annoying, so now we give her less to say. In fact, in succeeding shows, we toned down all of the harsh dialogue directed against Charlie Brown. We realized that

Lucy the psychiatrist.

what you read and what you hear are really separate things and do not come out the same way.

One of the big breakthroughs on the strip happened when Lucy opened her psychiatric booth. That got a lot of attention. It started off as a parody on lemonade stands. Lucy is a little different from the usual child: she went beyond lemonade stands and offered psychiatric help for five cents. It really went over. A Los Angeles psychiatrist, Benjamin Weininger, of the Southern California Counseling Center, sat in a lemonade stand offering the following: "In the Xmas Spirit . . . Counseling 5¢." He didn't know that Lucy raises her price to seven cents during the cold months.

Baby Linus.

7

Linus

Linus Van Pelt was a baby when he first appeared in the strip. At the time of his introduction, Lucy had been in the strip for about a year.

Linus expresses the stress put upon him by his family. For example, we have his always unseen grandmother, who hates his security blanket, and his mother, who puts notes in his lunch exhorting him to study hard.

Of all the things in the strip, I think that I am most proud of Linus's security blanket. I may not have invented the term, but I like to think that I helped make it a part of our language. I'm sure kids dragged around blankets before Linus appeared—I know mine did—but I'm sure he became the leading practitioner.

Speaking of my kids, here are a few more of the ideas that they have given me

Linus and Charlie Brown both have problems with Lucy, but Linus always has his old security blanket for comfort.

for the strip. Jill once said to me, "If you fold your hands upside down, you get the opposite of what you pray for."

Craig once pointed out that toothpaste made a great fingernail cleaner.

Amy was making a lot of noise at the dinner table one evening, and I finally said, "Amy, couldn't you be quiet for just a little while?" She became silent, picked up a piece of bread and began buttering it. Then she looked up and said, "Am I buttering too loud for you?"

These three things became tiny episodes of the strip that were starring roles

Linus is a kind boy, always trying to be helpful, but sometimes without much success.

for Linus.

Linus really comes to life around holiday time. One year he got ahead of himself and was looking for Christmas presents at Halloween time. Thus, instead of hoping to see Santa Claus, he came up with the idea of the Great Pumpkin.

I think that Halloween has always been one of my favorite days. I tend to like innocent holidays that don't pretend to be anything more than they are. I don't like holidays that separate people or segments of our society.

Schroeder is a much better musician than a baseball catcher, but he has the will to win.

8

Schroeder

Schroeder first appeared in the strip in 1951. He has had to contend with Lucy for nearly thirty years. When he first appeared, he was a baby, but I soon realized that there was nothing I could do with a baby in the strip so I very quickly had him grow up a bit and be able to walk around. He was named after another friend of mine who used to caddy with me at the Highland Park Golf Course in St. Paul. I can't re-member his first name. Perhaps I never knew it.

I guess that, at the time, I had decided to let Schroeder bring some classical music into the strip. My interest in music began one night when I was in the Army. We were watching a film on the life of George Gershwin, and I was taken with the beauti-ful music that he had written. Up until then, the only things that I had listened to were

Is Lucy a music lover…

the top ten songs on the Hit Parade.

One day I went out and bought a recording of Beethoven's Second Symphony and was so taken with it that I began to accumulate all the Beethoven symphonies. I then went on to Brahms, Mendelssohn and all the others. By that time, the first long-playing records had appeared, and my friends and I would get together in the evening and listen to each other's new albums. That was the way I developed an appreciation for music. It is amazing how much you can learn about

music just by reading the backs of album covers.

Music started in the strip when Schroeder was a baby. I was looking through a home study music book one day, and I noticed part of the score from Beethoven's Ninth Symphony. It seemed to me that it might be a good idea to let Charlie Brown sing some of the choral music from the final movement. I also thought that it might be funny if I had one of the kids play a toy piano accompaniment. My daughter, Meredith, had one that I used as a model.

or a Schroeder lover?

This gag was only supposed to last for a few days, but it turned out to be like the Red Baron series. I knew I had something so I kept it up, and now it has become part of my regular "theme and variations."

Those strips with Schroeder playing the piano and Lucy lounging against it are tedious to draw, however. The musical notes have to be accurate to make it unique.

I like to work in the little relationship between Schroeder and Lucy that shows another side of her character. Lucy bosses Charlie Brown and Linus around, but she is putty in the hands of Schroeder. On the other hand, without his piano, Schroeder is not all that impressive.

People often ask me, "Why did you pick Beethoven?" I guess all I can say is that the name Beethoven is funnier than Brahms. In addition, ask anyone to name a composer and the answer you get more times than not is "Beethoven."

Woodstock, like Snoopy, is a writer.

9

And All
The Others...

Although Woodstock really didn't appear as himself until 1970, he has been around since 1952. Way back then, I was drawing birds in the strip because I had thought up some funny incidents about birds that were flying past Snoopy's doghouse. But these birds were drawn rather realistically. Later, as I learned how to draw the characters better, I drew a couple of tiny birds that were hatched in a nest that was perched on Snoopy's stomach.

They were having a terrible time learning how to leave the nest because they couldn't fly properly. Snoopy was getting aggravated because he didn't think that he was ever going to get rid of them. As I drew them over and over, they began to take shape. One of them then became Snoopy's secretary because I had viewed

It is sometimes a struggle not to let Woodstock talk.

this little bird as a girl. For a while, I did secretary-and-boss ideas in the strip.

One day, I was reading an article in *Life* magazine about the Woodstock rock festival of 1969. That seemed to be a good name for the bird, but, of course, I had to make him a little boy bird. Snoopy and Woodstock have been fast friends ever since. I think that Woodstock has taken

The little bird's behavior isn't always perfect.

Woodstock finally gets named.

over some of the activities that Snoopy might have originally performed, so there must be a rapport between the two characters. That is not to say that they always get along together. There have been occasions when Snoopy called Woodstock "Feathers" and Woodstock irritatedly referred to Snoopy as "Banana Nose," but they are on good terms, even to the extent of Snoopy's taking out the other little birds—Conrad, Olivier and Bill—on Beagle Patrol Hikes. Now, there is another Patrol member—Harriet.

The Beagle Scout Troop in action.

What is more important than friendship?

Some of the Rerun gags are better without his appearing in the strip.

Over the years, all of the characters in the strip have grown up a little bit, at least until they bump their heads on the top of the panel or the balloon. Linus and Lucy also have a baby brother. Sometimes, I think he was a mistake.

Then there is Pig Pen, whose character is so restrictive that there is no reason for having him in the strip unless the idea has something to do with a kid who is always dirty. Usually I just run out of ideas for him, but somehow he keeps hanging in there.

Franklin, the black kid from the other side of town who shows up in Peppermint Patty's classroom, doesn't appear too much either. When I introduced him in

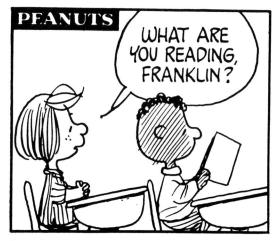

Peppermint Patty goes to school with Franklin.

1968, *Newsweek* magazine mentioned that it was great to find that Charlie Brown was not color blind.

There is a minor character named José Peterson who plays on Peppermint Patty's baseball team. He was the result of a dream I had about a character who was part Mexican and part Swedish.

Snoopy sometimes tries to get other people to protect him from the cat.

There are several characters in the strip who never appear. They are the adults, such as Miss Othmar, the teacher; Charlie Brown's father; and Linus's grandmother. I leave them out because they would make the strip too realistic. Besides, they might be too tall to fit in the panels.

The cat that threatens Snoopy is also never seen in the strip. When I first got the idea to give Snoopy an enemy, it seemed reasonable that the cat would appear as a character. Then I realized that if I had the cat appear, it would turn those episodes into the usual cat-and-dog cartoon strip.

Snoopy never learns.

Another problem would have been that the cat and the dog would have to talk to each other and, of course, Snoopy doesn't talk —he just thinks.

I also realized that I don't draw cats too well.

One day I took the cat out of the strip and made him an offstage presence. The cat works better that way in the same way that the little red-haired girl does. If I were to draw the cat now, I could not please many of the readers. Their imaginations have conjured up a mental picture of the cat that is much better than any I could draw.

Sally was a baby when she first appeared.

She works hard on her schoolwork.

Lucy's crabbiness has been important to the strip ever since it began, but I am glad that I gave Charlie Brown a little sister in 1959. I can switch from Lucy's being a fussbudget to Sally's school days and all the dumb reports that she gives. Sally stands for all the frustration and confusion that little kids experience at school. She is a favorite of many people because she is so uninhibited.

Peppermint Patty
never seems to
do well at school.

Then there is Peppermint Patty, who gets in trouble in school for completely different reasons. She is definitely one of my favorites, and I think that she could carry a whole strip by herself. Her name was inspired by my noticing a dish of candy that was sitting around the house.

Peppermint Patty is continually plagued with her D minuses in class—that's about the only grade she ever gets—and with falling asleep in school. She can't stay awake in class, and I get many letters from

Also, she has a
terrible time staying
awake in class.

people who are disturbed by this and feel that perhaps there is a medical problem involved.

I have hinted, however, about something in Patty's homelife. I have touched upon it lightly. She doesn't have a mother, and we don't know what happened to her mother. She is at home alone a lot of the time and seems to stay up late at night watching television. Maybe she is afraid to go to bed. Someday I may be able to solve that problem for her.

Patty seems to be made for the continued-strip sequences. One that I am quite proud of involved her feeling that she was not doing well in school and deciding that she would do better if she were in a private school. She investigated several schools, but couldn't find one that she could afford. Then Snoopy gave her a leaflet describing the Ace Obedience School. Patty enrolled and was proud of herself because she was doing so well, but she was puzzled because she could never

Marcie and Peppermint Patty are really the best of friends.

understand why everybody who came to the school brought their pets. She finally graduated and thought that she would never have to go back to school again. She was really disgusted when she found out that she had been in a dog obedience school and had to go back to human school.

Peppermint Patty came into the strip in the late 1960s. In the beginning, I created her because I needed somebody from another neighborhood to head up a team that would challenge Charlie Brown's baseball team. One summer, however, she went to camp, where she met Marcie.

I like the relationship that the two girls have. There is a real friendship there. They are different people, but they are both sincere little girls. Peppermint Patty goes through life with a set of blinders on. Marcie seems to have a better idea of what is going on around her. At any rate, she follows Patty around, constantly admiring her, doing whatever she says, until she

sees that Patty has gone too far in something. One other thing—I enjoy drawing them. Peppermint Patty and Marcie are as much fun to draw as Snoopy is.

I first created Marcie as one of those nameless campers who were exploring the outdoors and had Peppermint Patty as a camp monitor. All she did was to go to Patty's tent and tell her that her stomach

This was during the time when all the boys were beginning the long hair phase. I couldn't do it, though, because Marcie was already a girl and I had committed myself. I often think back on that narrow escape. I would have lost Marcie and I would have been selling out for a quick laugh.

My favorite sequence starring Patty and Marcie was also my longest. It lasted five weeks and eventually also became a TV show. Patty, who is lucky enough to have Snoopy as her ice skating instructor, decides that she wants to enter a skating competition. She needs a skating costume, which she cons Marcie into making. Protesting that she can't sew, Marcie goes on to prove it. The dress looks like a tent when Patty puts it on. Besides, Marcie has forgotten the sleeves. Marcie's mother then comes to the rescue and makes a nice dress for Patty.

Next, Patty decides that she needs her

hurt. I believe she called her "sir" out of misguided respect. The only thing that happened was that Peppermint Patty told Marcie to go to the nurse. It wasn't until I mailed in the strips that it occurred to me that it might have been funnier if Marcie—who was not yet named—was a boy and not a girl, and nobody knew the difference.

PEANUTS

I JUST REMEMBERED SOMETHING, SNOOPY...

I STILL OWE YOU FOR MY SKATING LESSONS, DON'T I?

WELL, I DON'T HAVE ANY MONEY, BUT I HAVE SOMETHING ELSE THAT I CAN GIVE YOU...

12-7   SCHULZ

I'm not too sure Snoopy's appearance was improved by the wig.

hair fixed and, once again, Marcie is nominated to do the job. This, too, is a mess. So Patty talks to Charlie Brown and convinces him that he should ask his barber father to try. Unfortunately, Charlie Brown forgot to tell his father that Patty was a girl, so she ends up with a horrible boy's haircut. There is only one thing left to do, and Patty does it. She gets a wig—an outlandish Orphan Annie-type wig.

Finally, she is ready for the skating competition. She shows up only to find out that it is not an ice skating contest, but a roller skating competition. The whole thing turns out happily. Peppermint Patty remembers that she hasn't paid Snoopy for coaching her, and she also realizes that she doesn't have any money to pay him, so with a gesture of magnanimity, she plants her new wig on poor Snoopy's head.

1950

1952

1959

1973

Charlie Brown's appearance has changed over the years...

10

Cartooning

All of us look different today from the way we did twenty years ago, and so do cartoon characters. It's not that the cartoonist is not trying to draw them the same all the time, it's just that he or she is trying to draw them as well as possible that day. We are rarely aware of the changes that occur.

I think that the future for comic strips is still unlimited. There will always be comic strips if newspaper editors are willing to tolerate them, but the success of the comic strip is entirely in the hands of these editors.

Of course, the directions in which we take comic strips in the future will depend on the amount of space that they give us for our drawings. We went through a bad period a few years ago when editors really trimmed the comic strips down to

1952   1959   1971

...and so has the appearance of the other characters.

atrocious minimum sizes, almost destroying some strips completely, but we seem to be bouncing back from that time. Theoretically, a comic strip artist has several people whom he has to please before his work is presented to the public. When you draw your six daily strips, you send them in to the newspaper syndicate whose job it is to market the strip and to distribute it.

By marketing, I mean that the feature must be sold to newspaper editors who subscribe to the service. By distributing, I mean that the syndicate must send the strip to the papers in time for them to publish the feature on the proper day.

The artist's job is to draw the strip on a regular schedule, send it to the syndicate and then keep on drawing it, maintaining at least the original quality, but always trying to improve. The first person who sees the strip when it arrives at the syndicate is the editor, and he or she checks it for spelling, for unsuitable material and for content. So the editor is the first person that the artist must please. Then the subscribing newspaper editors must be pleased or they will drop the strip. Finally, the reader must be pleased, and he or she is the person that the artist is really trying to make happy.

In cartooning, the first thing to develop is patience. There are no child prodigies in the field of comic strip art. This is probably because, in order to draw a strip, you have to have lived for a while. A cartoonist draws about those areas of life that he or she has observed. The young cartoonist, not having lived very long, usually draws cartoons of cartoons.

Abandon all thoughts of immediately becoming a syndicated cartoonist if you are still in your early teens. Try to draw for the school newspaper and develop your cartoon style; learn how to draw; go to art school; take life-drawing classes; develop a command of the English language; seek out a knowledge of good literature. Try to

1952

1959

1972

get a well-rounded education because that is the foundation for developing ideas.

If you are fortunate enough to be able to go to college, try to work for a college newspaper or any other kind of publication. Then be ready to submit cartoons to some of the smaller magazines. The names of these magazines are available in many authors' and writers' publications, or you can go to the library and thumb through magazines to see which ones of them publish the kind of cartoons that you are good at. Then just send them in—there is no trick to it.

Cartooning is one of the few areas where you don't really need an "in" to be published. You don't have to know anybody. In fact, knowing somebody is not going to help you at all. You still have to be able to draw funny cartoons in a way that no one else has done before.

Some people love driving so much that they are content to spend their lives behind the wheel of a truck. To many, this would seem intolerable. For others, cooking may be so fascinating that they are willing to spend all of their days in a kitchen, which would be completely contrary to the desires of many. Such it is with sitting at a drawing board.

If you are the sort of person who is restless or who loves to travel, then a lifetime sitting by yourself in a room at a drawing board is certainly not the place for you. Each of us seems to need a certain atmosphere to be at our best or to feel reasonably secure. The sailor longs for the open sea, while the farmer may actually tremble at the thought of venturing away from shore. Cartoonists may be similar to actors, who live through the imitation of others. These professions, of course, are very appealing because of the glamorous rewards that seem to be available, but it is the person who is able to stand the daily demands who succeeds. Or, rather, it is the person who is so obsessed with what he is doing that he really cannot

1952   1959   1972

stop—who draws, acts or writes until he succeeds.

There seem to be many unrecognized but necessary abilities to sustain the creation of a daily comic strip. I think "sustain" is a good word to use to describe the process, for it is no great accomplishment to draw a few cartoons, and it is not much harder to draw a simple gag each day, but it is very, very difficult to sustain a high quality day after day, month after month, and year after year. For example, a comic strip artist must take into consideration the twenty-four hours that go by between the time the reader sees one strip and when the next one appears. This is important to consider when you are doing even a simple story.

The most difficult and sometimes almost impossible task is to be able to judge whether what you have done is actually funny. I have often wanted to make a collection of what I call "non-gags," but somehow have never gotten started. Non-gags are strips drawn by a cartoonist who, like all of us, has on a

certain day lost the ability to decide whether what he has drawn is funny. Unfortunately, on that day he makes the wrong judgment and turns in a "non-gag"—a strip that is not only weak or flat, but just plain "nothing." It takes a light touch to turn out good work, and only the rare person with "sustaining" ability can function on the days when the "light touch" is not quite there.

If you have been in a group where one person was louder and more boisterous than the rest, you will know how dominating one form of humor can be over another. This is one more problem that faces the comic strip. Some features do not belong on the same page with others. An adventure strip with intricate detail can be overwhelmed by easy-to-read gag strips, and a gentle strip can be destroyed by being forced to share space with cruder types, for the reader will always have difficulty shifting mental gears as he reads down the page.

I have never been concerned about work materials as I should have, but I do

1959   1969

know that an aspiring cartoonist should seek out good quality pens, brushes, ink and paper in order not to be discouraged by poor results because of inadequate material. When I was of high school age, I used to be frustrated in my pen-and-ink efforts because I was trying to draw on the pieces of white cardboard that came with my dad's shirts from the laundry. This paper had a center filling that was soft, and the ink did not take properly on the surface. Later, of course, I discovered what the proper drawing papers were, and it was an event for me to go downtown and buy two large sheets of Strathmore (which was all I could afford) and then return home and cut them into strips. I refuse even to talk about the kind of pens I use, because I don't want some young person to think there is something magic about a certain type. Each person has to find the kind that suits his or her drawing style or technique.

When you reach your mid-twenties, you are ready to begin trying to develop a style and to invent some characters that can sustain themselves over the years. Don't expect instant success. You will have to learn to deal with that fact of life—the rejection slip. Rejection slips are coldhearted. They don't tell you anything except that you have failed. They don't tell you why.

If you are getting nothing but rejections, it may be that your work is worthless. If your work has some value, you may get an occasional letter from an editor saying that he or she regrets the rejection, and telling you the reason why the cartoon was not bought. As you get closer to selling your work, you will find that the rejections get a little less harsh. Then you will know that you may make it someday.

The cartooning field actually is wide open for anyone who has something special to offer, and this is especially true for women. Syndicates are always looking for female artists who have a different approach with their drawing and humor.

11

My Day

I like cartooning because I can think of something, draw it and send it in without having to check with a committee and argue over whether an idea is funny enough.

A comic strip is like a repertory company. You have a group of players, and when it is time to cast a play you work with the actors you have. The most important element in keeping a comic strip alive and sustaining it over a long period of time is having good characters. The lead character generally has attributes which are similar to other lead characters. If you have a good basic character, he or she can put up with the extreme characters that populate the strip. The main character must be someone whom people care about.

Drawing style is far more important than

Oh, the horror of unrequited love.

many people realize. There is room for extreme caricature and radical style in gag cartooning and political cartooning, but rarely in comic strips. The audience must be able to recognize immediately the expression that is on a character's face. This means that the drawing style must be relatively subdued. A cartoonist must also try to go into areas where other media cannot go.

As far as my daily schedule is concerned, I rarely get up before eight in the morning. I would like to be the type of person who did rise early and accomplish great things before noon, and I have great admiration for people who get up early and work in

On the other hand, kindness can come from the strangest places.

their gardens and plow the fields and do that sort of thing, but it's not me. If I get up too early, I fall asleep at the drawing board.

Actually, there is no reason for me to get up early. I can never get started until I have looked over the morning mail, and that doesn't get to the studio until about nine. The mail kind of sets the tone for what I have to do during the day. The secretaries usually go through and distribute the mail. Some things having to do with business go to one place, and other things having to do with licensing go to another, but I get the personal mail. One of the best things about being a cartoonist is the interesting mail you get, and I always look forward to the

opening of the letters.

Drawing a comic strip requires a great amount of discipline. This means not only the discipline of getting the work done, but also the discipline of trying to get better all the time. I maintain a regular schedule because I have found that having an irregular schedule leads to fuzzy thinking. I have to work at the job five days a week during regular working hours to produce my best work. If I get far enough ahead to take off for a week to go somewhere, it takes me two or three days to get back on the track once I get home. This is always disturbing.

I've learned to live with it, however, and I know that even if I am gone for a week, I will probably get an idea for the strip so that when I get back I will have something to draw. Sometimes I leave an idea on my desk just before I go away so that I can get started immediately on the Monday morning of my return.

When five o'clock comes, I leave the studio. I've never allowed my work to interfere with my homelife. I've never said, "No, we can't go to the movies tonight because I've got work to do."

I have a desk which I try desperately to keep clear. I have a dread of things being hidden under other things that won't get attended to for a while. I also hate to have a stack of things on one side of the desk that interfere with the drawing of the strip. The main purpose of the desk is to have a place where I can line up the strips after I have finished working on them. I am frequently working on four or five strips at the same time, since I don't usually start a strip and finish it completely on the same day.

I may do the lettering first and then set it

Sitting at the old drawing board. (R. Smith Kiliper photo)

aside and try to think of another idea. If I get another idea, I will do the lettering on that strip and also set it aside. When I find that I am not going to get any more ideas that day, I go back to the lettered strips and start to finish them. Therefore, I always have these partial strips lined up on the desk until all six of them are done. Then I may look at them and rearrange them, thinking that one should be the Monday strip instead of the Thursday strip, and so on. The deadline for the strips to be received in the offices of the syndicate in New York is six weeks in advance of

The "Peanuts" gang can be creative, too.

publication, but I try to stay ahead of that.

Each of my daily strips is done in four panels. I draw them on rectangular paper that is five inches high and twenty inches long, so that each panel is five inches by five inches.

When I color a Sunday page, all I am doing is coloring in the squares as if I were working on a coloring book. I have a photostat of the strip in black and white, and I just color it in with colored pencils. There is a chart with sixty-four various shades of color, and they are numbered, so if I want Charlie Brown's sweater to be bright red, I just use the numbered pencil that corresponds to the chart color that I want.

The basic problem for any comic strip artist is coming up with ideas. Doing a strip is something like having to do a term paper every day. Some days the ideas come quickly, other days they don't come at all.

Frankly, most ideas come to me after I have forced myself to sit down and think cold-bloodedly. A cartoonist has to be able to take a blank sheet of paper and sit down in a room by himself and force ideas to come.

There are mechanical ways of doing this that all cartoonists develop. The most obvious one is to put one of the characters

Sometimes I have to think for quite a while before I come up with an idea.
(R. Smith Kiliper photo)

in a situation where he or she doesn't belong, or put an object in an unfamiliar situation, but these are mechanical ways, and they produce only mechanical ideas.

I try to use a lot of sight humor because cartooning is obviously drawing funny pictures and, because of that, there is no other business that can compete with it. Even live actors cannot compete with a funny drawing, although they can compete with a strip that relies on verbal humor.

The question "What do you do when you have writer's block?" is an amateur's question. The professional has no time for

The studio. (R. Smith Kiliper photo)

writer's block, because the newspapers come out every day.

My big concern is leveling off in my work. This has happened to other artists— their strip levels off and stops breaking new ground. I believe that this won't happen to an artist if he or she retains the ability to be interesting personally, and keeps an interest in other people and what they do, and in their surroundings. This interest can be translated into the drawings and can help the artist's feature to continue to grow.

My nice place to draw. (R. Smith Kiliper photo)

I've always found it difficult to talk about the characters in the "Peanuts" strip. I think that this is because I draw them, and if I have to talk about them, I have failed in the drawing. I would much rather have the reader draw his own conclusions or analyze the characters without help from me. It always delights me when someone says that he got a certain thought from a comic strip that I drew, even if it didn't happen to be the thought that I intended. That doesn't matter.

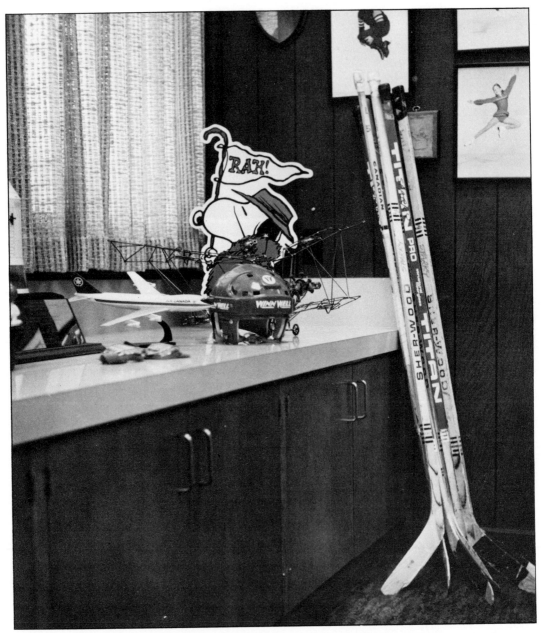

Here's a little corner of the office showing some of my souvenirs.
Notice the beat-up hockey sticks. (R. Smith Kiliper photo)

I once heard of a man who would stop people on the street and say "What's your excuse for cluttering up the earth?" This is a harsh question, but we all ask it of ourselves in different ways many times throughout our lives. A person who is able to contribute something to the world is a fortunate person, and each of us should be able at least to "brighten the corner" where we are. Drawing funny pictures is a form of contribution if the creator does not take himself too seriously. We don't live in a very secure world, and we need help from one another in countless ways. None of us knows how long we are going to live or under what circumstances, but being able to laugh at this condition is a blessing that has surely helped mankind to survive. Cartooning is hard work sometimes, but at least one has the satisfaction of knowing he has made others laugh.

As Charlie Brown's sister, Sally, has said, "It's also better than standing in the rain."

Appendix:
Some Things I'm Proud Of

1950   "Peanuts" appears for the first time.
1952   The first "Peanuts" book is published.
1955   Winner of the "Reuben" award of the National Cartoonists Society.
1958   Winner of the "Humorist of the Year" award from Yale University.
1960   Winner of the "School Bell" award from the National Education Association.
1962   Winner of the "Best Humor Strip of the Year" award of

the National Cartoonists Society.

1963 Awarded an honorary doctorate by Anderson College in Indiana.

1964 Winner of a second "Reuben" award of the National Cartoonists Society.

1965 "A Charlie Brown Christmas" wins both an Emmy and a Peabody award.

1966 Awarded a Doctor of Humane Letters degree by St. Mary's College in California.

1967 Awarded a Certificate of Merit from the Art Director's Club of New York. Charles M. Schulz Day proclaimed in California by Governor Reagan. *You're a Good Man, Charlie Brown* opens in New York.

1968 The ice rink in Santa Rosa opens.

1969 Charlie Brown and Snoopy named mascots of the Apollo 10 crew. *A Boy Named Charlie Brown* nominated for an Academy Award.

1970 Snoopy joins the Ice Follies.

1971 Received the key to the city of San Diego on Peanuts Day. Snoopy joins Holiday on Ice.

1973 Received the Big Brother of the Year award. *You're a Good Man, Charlie Brown* appears on the Hallmark Hall of Fame television special.

1974 "A Charlie Brown Thanksgiving" wins an Emmy. Named Grand Marshal of the Rose Bowl Parade.

1978 Named Cartoonist of the Year by the International Pavilion of Humor of Montreal.

1979 Named National Chairman of the 1979 Christmas Seal campaign.

Index

Charles Monroe Schulz was born in Minneapolis and lived in the state of Minnesota until he entered the Army in 1943. He first studied cartooning by taking a correspondence course with "Art Instruction Schools" and began his career as a free-lance cartoonist. Today he is known and loved by millions of people for his famous comic strip. His "Peanuts" characters delight readers in more than two thousand newspapers around the world and charm audiences of network television specials and feature films. He has received honorary degrees as well as many prestigious awards, and was named Grand Marshal of the 1974 Rose Bowl Parade and National Chairman of the 1979 Christmas Seal campaign. Mr. Schulz lives in Santa Rosa, California.